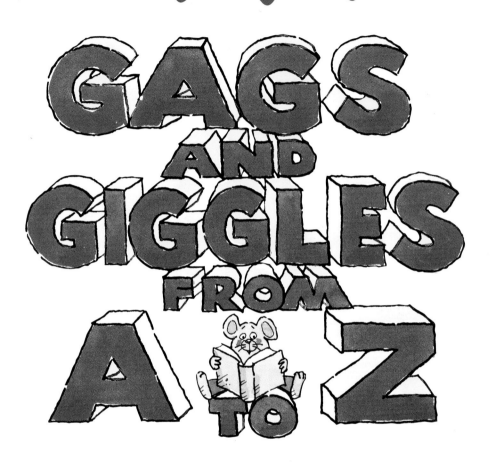

GAGS AND GIGGLES FROM A TO Z

by Diane Namm
illustrated by Wayne Becker

STERLING

New York / London
www.sterlingpublishing.com/kids

STERLING and the distinctive Sterling logo are registered trademarks
of Sterling Publishing Co., Inc.

Library of Congress Cataloging-in-Publication Data

Namm, Diane.
Gags and giggles from A to Z / Diane Namm, illustrated by Wayne Becker.
p. cm. -- (Laugh-a-long readers)
ISBN-13: 978-1-4027-5000-7
ISBN-10: 1-4027-5000-5
1. Wit and humor, Juvenile. I. Becker, Wayne. II. Title.
PN6166.N34 2008
818'.5402--dc22
2007030242

2 4 6 8 10 9 7 5 3 1

Published 2008 by Sterling Publishing Co., Inc.
387 Park Avenue South, New York, NY 10016
Originally published and © 2004 by Barnes and Noble, Inc.
Distributed in Canada by Sterling Publishing
c/o Canadian Manda Group, 165 Dufferin Street
Toronto, Ontario, Canada M6K 3H6
Distributed in the United Kingdom by GMC Distribution Services
Castle Place, 166 High Street, Lewes, East Sussex, England BN7 1XU
Distributed in Australia by Capricorn Link (Australia) Pty. Ltd.
P.O. Box 704, Windsor, NSW 2756, Australia

Written by Diane Namm
Illustrated by Wayne Becker
Designed by Jo Obarowski

Sterling ISBN-13: 978-1-4027-5000-7
ISBN-10: 1-4027-5000-5

For information about custom editions, special sales, premium and corporate purchases,
please contact Sterling Special Sales Department at 800-805-5489 or specialsales@sterlingpub.com.

What has four eyes but cannot see?

Mississippi.

What is the longest word?

Post office. It has the most letters.

What is in December that is not in any other month?

The letter D.

What seven letters did the girl say to her closet?

O I C U R M T.

What is the best thing to wear
to a tea party?

A T-shirt.

What is in the middle of earth?

The letter R.

What appears once in a second,
twice in a week, and once in a year?

The letter E.

How do you make seven even?

Take away the S.

What starts with T, ends with T, and is full of T?

A teapot.

If all the letters of the alphabet were invited to tea, which ones would be late?

U, V, W, X, Y, and Z—
they all come after T.

What letter is also a bug?

The letter B.

Which two letters does a skunk like best?

P U!

How do you make oil boil?

Add the letter B.

What goes from Z to A?

A zebra.

What letters can a bear catch in his sleep?

ZZZZZZZZZZZZZZZZS.